TALES FROM MAD LIBS®

THE GOOD, THE BAD, AND THE

Itchy
ADJECTIVE

BY GABE SORIA

MAD LIBS
An Imprint of Penguin Random House LLC, New York

Mad Libs format and text copyright © 2020 by Penguin Random House LLC. All rights reserved.

Concept created by Roger Price & Leonard Stern

Cover illustration by Scott Brooks

Published by Mad Libs,
an imprint of Penguin Random House LLC, New York.
Printed in the USA.

Visit us online at www.penguinrandomhouse.com.

ISBN 9781524793579
1 3 5 7 9 10 8 6 4 2

MAD LIBS

INSTRUCTIONS

MAD LIBS® is a game for people who don't like games! It can be played by one, two, three, four, or forty.

• RIDICULOUSLY SIMPLE DIRECTIONS

In this book you will find a story containing blank spaces where words are left out. One player, the READER, asks the other players, the WRITERS, to give him/her words. These words are used to fill in the blank spaces in the story.

• TO PLAY

The READER asks each WRITER in turn to call out a word—an adjective or a noun or whatever the space calls for—and uses them to fill in the blank spaces in the story. The result is a MAD LIBS® game.

When the READER then reads the completed MAD LIBS® game to the other players, they will discover that they have written a story that is fantastic, screamingly funny, shocking, silly, crazy, or just plain dumb—depending upon which words each WRITER called out.

• EXAMPLE (Before and After)

" _____ !" he said _____
      EXCLAMATION   ADVERB

as he jumped into his convertible _____ and
                                              NOUN

drove off with his _____ wife.
                          ADJECTIVE

" __OUCH__ !" he said __HAPPILY__
      EXCLAMATION   ADVERB

as he jumped into his convertible __CAT__ and
                                              NOUN

drove off with his __BRAVE__ wife.
                          ADJECTIVE

MAD⊙LIBS®
QUICK REVIEW

In case you have forgotten what adjectives, adverbs, nouns, and verbs are, here is a quick review:

An ADJECTIVE describes something or somebody. *Lumpy*, *soft*, *ugly*, *messy*, and *short* are adjectives.

An ADVERB tells how something is done. It modifies a verb and usually ends in "ly." *Modestly*, *stupidly*, *greedily*, and *carefully* are adverbs.

A NOUN is the name of a person, place, or thing. *Sidewalk*, *umbrella*, *bridle*, *bathtub*, and *nose* are nouns.

A VERB is an action word. *Run*, *pitch*, *jump*, and *swim* are verbs. Put the verbs in past tense if the directions say PAST TENSE. *Ran*, *pitched*, *jumped*, and *swam* are verbs in the past tense.

When we ask for A PLACE, we mean any sort of place: a country or city (*Spain*, *Cleveland*) or a room (*bathroom*, *kitchen*).

An EXCLAMATION or SILLY WORD is any sort of funny sound, gasp, grunt, or outcry, like *Wow!*, *Ouch!*, *Whomp!*, *Ick!*, and *Gadzooks!*

When we ask for specific words, like a NUMBER, a COLOR, an ANIMAL, or a PART OF THE BODY, we mean a word that is one of those things, like *seven*, *blue*, *horse*, or *head*.

When we ask for a PLURAL, it means more than one. For example, *cat* pluralized is *cats*.

MAD LIBS® is fun to play with friends, but you can also play it by yourself! To begin with, DO NOT look at the chapter on the next page. Fill in the blanks on this page with the words called for. Then, using the words you have selected, fill in the blank spaces in the chapter.

Now you've created your own hilarious MAD LIBS® game!

CHAPTER 1:
CAMPFIRE TALES

ADJECTIVE _____

SILLY WORD _____

ANIMAL (PLURAL) _____

NOUN _____

EXCLAMATION _____

A PLACE _____

PART OF THE BODY _____

VERB _____

ADJECTIVE _____

ADVERB _____

TYPE OF FOOD _____

ADJECTIVE _____

OCCUPATION (PLURAL) _____

TYPE OF LIQUID _____

VERB _____

ADJECTIVE _____

NOUN _____

ADJECTIVE _____

CHAPTER 1:
CAMPFIRE TALES

It had been a hard, _____ day on the _____ trail.
(ADJECTIVE) *happy / focused* · (SILLY WORD) *poorna / unkaduboonka*

The cowboys drove a herd of _____ across the dry plains,
(ANIMAL (PLURAL)) *lizard / cats*

kicking up _____ along the way as they looked for somewhere
(NOUN) *lego / chair*

to bed down.

"_____!" one of the cowboys said when they came
(EXCLAMATION) *Oh my / Oh what*

across a gritty cowgirl at a lonely campsite. The _____ looked
(A PLACE) *Barkers Island / is*

as good a place as any to grab some shut-_____. Besides, it
(PART OF THE BODY) *eye / stomach*

was quitting time, time to _____ the horses and eat some
(VERB) *walk / toot*

grub.

"That food sure smells _____," said one of the cowboys to
(ADJECTIVE) *sleep / stinky*

the cowgirl as she _____ stirred a pot of _____ over
(ADVERB) *slowly / quickly* · (TYPE OF FOOD) *pizza*

the fire.

"Gather 'round, you _____-for-nothing _____,
(ADJECTIVE) *cheery / concentrating* · (OCCUPATION (PLURAL)) *doctors / cherries / presidents*

and grab yourself some stew and a hot cup of _____. I'm
(TYPE OF LIQUID) *water*

gonna _____ you a tale of the _____ West. And it all
(VERB) *blast / fast* · (ADJECTIVE)

starts with a song I learned on this here _____—a song about
(NOUN) *house / park*

the Good, the Bad, and the _____."
(ADJECTIVE) *stinky / bright*

MAD LIBS® is fun to play with friends, but you can also play it by yourself! To begin with, DO NOT look at the chapter on the next page. Fill in the blanks on this page with the words called for. Then, using the words you have selected, fill in the blank spaces in the chapter.

Now you've created your own hilarious MAD LIBS® game!

CHAPTER 2:
THE BALLAD OF GOPHER GULCH

ADVERB _____

NOUN _____

ADJECTIVE _____

NUMBER _____

VERB (PAST TENSE) _____

ANIMAL _____

VERB _____

ADJECTIVE _____

A PLACE (PLURAL) _____

OCCUPATION (PLURAL) _____

ADJECTIVE _____

ANIMAL _____

ADJECTIVE _____

PART OF THE BODY (PLURAL) _____

ADJECTIVE _____

NOUN _____

SILLY WORD _____

CHAPTER 2:
THE BALLAD OF GOPHER GULCH

The cowgirl squinted __Quickly__ at the cowboys as __Gum__
                ADVERB   NOUN

wafted up from the fire that was billowing into the __slow__
                                                 ADJECTIVE

night air. Then she strummed her __2,024__ -string guitar and
                                    NUMBER

__ran__ her song . . .
VERB (PAST TENSE)

Come 'round, all you __Wolf spider__ -boys,
                           ANIMAL

and __run__ to my tale
          VERB

of __louse__ days and dirty __Disneylands__
     ADJECTIVE   A PLACE (PLURAL)

and __bike pros__ in jail!
       OCCUPATION (PLURAL)

It's a tale as __creepy__ as time,
           ADJECTIVE

and one that's full of danger,

about the town of __spider__ Gulch
               ANIMAL

and a/an __Greatest__ stranger!
           ADJECTIVE

So, let me bend your __Buttchecks__
          PART OF THE BODY (PLURAL)

for a while, my __Stinky__ friends.
         ADJECTIVE

'Cause this is a/an __Balloon__ from long ago,
          NOUN

and here's how it begins! __pee pee__ -haw!
          SILLY WORD

MAD LIBS® is fun to play with friends, but you can also play it by yourself! To begin with, DO NOT look at the chapter on the next page. Fill in the blanks on this page with the words called for. Then, using the words you have selected, fill in the blank spaces in the chapter.

Now you've created your own hilarious MAD LIBS® game!

CHAPTER 3:
THE STAGECOACH TO GOPHER GULCH

VERB (PAST TENSE) _____

NOUN _____

ADJECTIVE _____

SILLY WORD _____

ADJECTIVE _____

OCCUPATION (PLURAL) _____

ANIMAL (PLURAL) _____

VERB ENDING IN "ING" _____

EXCLAMATION _____

ANIMAL (PLURAL) _____

NOUN _____

VERB (PAST TENSE) _____

VERB _____

TYPE OF CONTAINER _____

ADJECTIVE _____

PLURAL NOUN _____

NOUN _____

VERB _____

CHAPTER 3:
THE STAGECOACH TO GOPHER GULCH

It all ___cheated___ in the town of Gopher ___bacteria___,
VERB (PAST TENSE)   NOUN

the most ___vile___ town this side of the ___Gubernatorial___ River.
ADJECTIVE   SILLY WORD

For years, the ___filthy___ people of the town lived in fear of a gang
ADJECTIVE

of ___plumbers___ that robbed its banks and rustled its
OCCUPATION (PLURAL)

___goats___. But all of that changed the day a stranger came
ANIMAL (PLURAL)

___barfing___ into town.
VERB ENDING IN "ING"

The stranger lurched forward when her stagecoach driver shouted,

"___woo kooh___!" at the team of ___porpoises___ that pulled
EXCLAMATION   ANIMAL (PLURAL)

them across the dusty trail. "That there is Gopher Gulch," said the

driver with ___covid-19___ in his voice.
NOUN

The stranger ___infected___ into the distance. "It doesn't
VERB (PAST TENSE)

___heal___ so bad to me," she said.
VERB

"Okay. But don't say I didn't warn ya, stranger. That place is more

trouble than a/an ___handlebar bag___ full of ___green___
TYPE OF CONTAINER   ADJECTIVE

___pizzas___." The lonesome stranger nodded at the
PLURAL NOUN

___cake___-coach driver, and they began to ___crawl___ toward
NOUN   VERB

Gopher Gulch.

MAD LIBS® is fun to play with friends, but you can also play it by yourself! To begin with, DO NOT look at the chapter on the next page. Fill in the blanks on this page with the words called for. Then, using the words you have selected, fill in the blank spaces in the chapter.

Now you've created your own hilarious MAD LIBS® game!

CHAPTER 4:
AT THE GOPHER SALOON

NOUN _____

VERB (PAST TENSE) _____

ARTICLE OF CLOTHING _____

PLURAL NOUN _____

ADJECTIVE _____

NOUN _____

VERB ENDING IN "ING" _____

ADJECTIVE _____

COLOR _____

ARTICLE OF CLOTHING _____

NOUN _____

TYPE OF LIQUID _____

EXCLAMATION _____

ADJECTIVE _____

OCCUPATION _____

PART OF THE BODY _____

CHAPTER 4:
AT THE GOPHER SALOON

A tumble-_pillow_ NOUN rolled swiftly past as the stranger _swam_ VERB (PAST TENSE) down Main Street, with the spurs on her _____ ARTICLE OF CLOTHING clinking as she went. The _F_____ PLURAL NOUN of the town stared at the stranger. She looked lean, mean, and _whietes_ ADJECTIVE. Then, the stranger heard the sound of _chair_ NOUN coming from the saloon, so she pushed her way through the _walking_ VERB ENDING IN "ING" doors. The stranger made her way through the crowded saloon until she reached the _coletful_ ADJECTIVE bar.

An old man wearing a/an _pink_ COLOR _sock_ ARTICLE OF CLOTHING greeted her. "What can I get ya, stranger?" asked the _tails_ NOUN-tender. "_milk_ TYPE OF LIQUID," said the stranger, her throat parched. Then a loud "_zots_ EXCLAMATION" broke the silence. The stranger looked up to see a dirty and _soft_ ADJECTIVE _knoel_ OCCUPATION standing in the entrance of the saloon. It was none other than Wild Bob.

The notorious outlaw pointed his _pillow_ PART OF THE BODY at the stranger. "I'm talking to YOU," he said with a snarl.

MAD LIBS® is fun to play with friends, but you can also play it by yourself! To begin with, DO NOT look at the chapter on the next page. Fill in the blanks on this page with the words called for. Then, using the words you have selected, fill in the blank spaces in the chapter.

Now you've created your own hilarious MAD LIBS® game!

CHAPTER 5:
THE BRAWL

PLURAL NOUN _____

ARTICLE OF CLOTHING _____

VERB (PAST TENSE) _____

ADJECTIVE _____

ANIMAL (PLURAL) _____

A PLACE _____

EXCLAMATION _____

PART OF THE BODY _____

VERB ENDING IN "ING" _____

VERB _____

ADJECTIVE _____

NOUN _____

PART OF THE BODY _____

ADJECTIVE _____

TYPE OF CONTAINER _____

SILLY WORD _____

VERB ENDING IN "ING" _____

VERB (PAST TENSE) _____

CHAPTER 5:
THE BRAWL

"We don't take much to strangers 'round these _____," *[PLURAL NOUN]*
said Wild Bob from behind the _____ *[ARTICLE OF CLOTHING]* covering his
face, as he _____ *[VERB (PAST TENSE)]* over to the stranger. "Especially
_____ *[ADJECTIVE]* _____ *[ANIMAL (PLURAL)]* like you." There was nervous
laughter inside (the) _____ *[A PLACE]* at the outlaw's joke.

"_____, *[EXCLAMATION]* and you're nothin' but a/an _____ *[PART OF THE BODY]* -less
rattlesnake," said the stranger.

"Them's _____ *[VERB ENDING IN "ING"]* words!" cried Wild Bob. "Let's
_____ *[VERB]* this outside!"

Moments later, the _____ *[ADJECTIVE]* stranger and Wild Bob faced off in
the middle of the street. It was so still, you could hear a/an _____ *[NOUN]*
drop. Wild Bob tried to put the stranger in a/an _____ *[PART OF THE BODY]* -lock,
but the stranger was too _____ *[ADJECTIVE]* for him. She dodged the
outlaw, and he fell back into the horse's watering _____. *[TYPE OF CONTAINER]*
The crowd laughed as Wild Bob yelped, "_____!" *[SILLY WORD]* He was
_____ *[VERB ENDING IN "ING"]* wet. "This ain't over!" _____ *[VERB (PAST TENSE)]* the
embarrassed outlaw before disappearing down the alleyway.

MAD LIBS® is fun to play with friends, but you can also play it by yourself! To begin with, DO NOT look at the chapter on the next page. Fill in the blanks on this page with the words called for. Then, using the words you have selected, fill in the blank spaces in the chapter.

Now you've created your own hilarious MAD LIBS® game!

CHAPTER 6:
THERE'S A NEW SHERIFF IN TOWN

VERB (PAST TENSE) _____

EXCLAMATION _____

ANIMAL _____

A PLACE _____

PERSON IN ROOM _____

TYPE OF BUILDING _____

PART OF THE BODY _____

VERB (PAST TENSE) _____

PLURAL NOUN _____

ARTICLE OF CLOTHING _____

ADJECTIVE _____

COLOR _____

NOUN _____

VERB (PAST TENSE) _____

NOUN _____

OCCUPATION _____

CHAPTER 6:
THERE'S A NEW SHERIFF IN TOWN

As the outlaw _skying_ out of town, the citizens

VERB (PAST TENSE)

cheered, "_wowsos_!" It had been a/an _a intes_ age

EXCLAMATION   ANIMAL

since anyone had stood up to any of the outlaws plaguing (the)

f Loth. The mayor of Gopher Gulch, _Oliver_,

A PLACE   PERSON IN ROOM

watched all of this through the window of his office in the town

post office and soon got the beginnings of an idea in his

TYPE OF BUILDING

Armpit. He exited his office and _swam_

PART OF THE BODY   VERB (PAST TENSE)

into the street.

Once there, he ran to the stranger, who was surrounded by cheering

cat. The mayor reached into the pocket of his

PLURAL NOUN

pant and took out a/an _cheat ful_ object:

ARTICLE OF CLOTHING   ADJECTIVE

a/an _purple_ star that had the words "Gopher Gulch

COLOR

mountin etched into its surface. He _an_

NOUN   VERB (PAST TENSE)

the _pizza_ into the stranger's hand. "Stranger," said the mayor,

NOUN

"I'd like to be the first to congratulate you on your new job! From now

on, you'll be known as the _mailman_ of Gopher Gulch."

OCCUPATION

MAD LIBS® is fun to play with friends, but you can also play it by yourself! To begin with, DO NOT look at the chapter on the next page. Fill in the blanks on this page with the words called for. Then, using the words you have selected, fill in the blank spaces in the chapter.

Now you've created your own hilarious MAD LIBS® game!

CHAPTER 7:
GOPHER GULCH'S MOST WANTED

PART OF THE BODY _____

OCCUPATION _____

NOUN _____

ADVERB _____

PART OF THE BODY _____

SILLY WORD _____

NUMBER _____

NOUN _____

NOUN _____

NOUN _____

VERB ENDING IN "ING" _____

NUMBER _____

ARTICLE OF CLOTHING _____

CHAPTER 7:
GOPHER GULCH'S MOST WANTED

The new sheriff shook the mayor's ___belly button___ , and they both

walked to the ___Athek___ 's office on the other side of the street.
_{OCCUPATION}

Inside, a young man sat with his head down on the wooden

___watch___ , snoring ___happily___ in the afternoon heat. The
_{NOUN}   _{ADVERB}

mayor cleared his ___whisker___ and said, "___uohyoat___," and the
_{PART OF THE BODY}   _{SILLY WORD}

man jumped. "John, this is the new sheriff. Sheriff, this is Deputy

John, your number ___74___ -in-command."
_{NUMBER}

The sheriff and deputy shook hands. "I'm so glad you're here," said

Deputy John. "We're in a fix here in Gopher Gulch, and that there

___itchy___ is the main culprit." Deputy John pointed to a poster
_{NOUN}

on the wall that read:

WANTED: WILD BOB, for the crimes against ___wagen___
_{NOUN}

and ___flower___ **, not to mention cattle** ___serching___ !
_{NOUN}   _{VERB ENDING IN "ING"}

Reward: $ ___itchty___ .
_{NUMBER}

The sheriff was quiet for a moment. Then she pinned the gold star

on her ___ynie___ .
_{ARTICLE OF CLOTHING}

MAD LIBS® is fun to play with friends, but you can also play it by yourself! To begin with, DO NOT look at the chapter on the next page. Fill in the blanks on this page with the words called for. Then, using the words you have selected, fill in the blank spaces in the chapter.

Now you've created your own hilarious MAD LIBS® game!

CHAPTER 8:
THE BALLAD OF GOPHER GULCH, PART 2

TYPE OF LIQUID _____

VERB _____

PLURAL NOUN _____

NOUN _____

PART OF THE BODY (PLURAL) _____

ADJECTIVE _____

NOUN _____

VERB _____

OCCUPATION _____

ADJECTIVE _____

ADJECTIVE _____

NOUN _____

VERB ENDING IN "ING" _____

VERB (PAST TENSE) _____

VERB (PAST TENSE) _____

ADJECTIVE _____

CHAPTER 8:
THE BALLAD OF GOPHER GULCH, PART 2

Back at the campsite, the gritty cowgirl paused to take a sip of her

steaming __lemonade__ . "That sheriff sure don't __look__
TYPE OF LIQUID   VERB

much," said one of the cowboys.

"You __hooks__ want to hear this story or not?" the cowgirl
PLURAL NOUN

asked her captive __investigator__ . The cowboys all shut their
NOUN

__feet__ quick after that. "Okay, then," said the
PART OF THE BODY (PLURAL)

__smelly__ cowgirl as she strummed her __kangaroo__ and began
ADJECTIVE   NOUN

to __fart__ her song . . .
VERB

Now the sheriff and __farmer__ John
OCCUPATION

had a/an __bright__ job to do!
ADJECTIVE

The streets were __dark__ , the bank was in __color__ ,
ADJECTIVE   NOUN

and some cattle were __farting__ , too!
VERB ENDING IN "ING"

So they __farted__ up the streets
VERB (PAST TENSE)

and __smelled__ order straight away!
VERB (PAST TENSE)

But those __cushiony__ outlaws were still hiding about,
ADJECTIVE

and they weren't goin' away!

MAD LIBS® is fun to play with friends, but you can also play it by yourself! To begin with, DO NOT look at the chapter on the next page. Fill in the blanks on this page with the words called for. Then, using the words you have selected, fill in the blank spaces in the chapter.

Now you've created your own hilarious MAD LIBS® game!

CHAPTER 9:
A FEW WEEKS LATER . . .

VERB (PAST TENSE) _____

NOUN _____

VERB ENDING IN "ING" _____

ADJECTIVE _____

OCCUPATION (PLURAL) _____

VERB ENDING IN "ING" _____

ADJECTIVE _____

VERB ENDING IN "ING" _____

VERB ENDING IN "ING" _____

ADJECTIVE _____

VERB _____

PART OF THE BODY (PLURAL) _____

ADJECTIVE _____

A PLACE _____

PLURAL NOUN _____

ANIMAL (PLURAL) _____

CHAPTER 9:
A FEW WEEKS LATER . . .

Time ___Ran___ in Gopher Gulch, but before long, the
            VERB (PAST TENSE)

sheriff and Deputy John had restored safety and ___Pie___ to the
                                                    NOUN

town. They started by ___looking___ lots of ___left___ Bob's
                       VERB ENDING IN "ING"   ADJECTIVE

low-ranking ___mailmen___. That meant ___walking___
            OCCUPATION (PLURAL)   VERB ENDING IN "ING"

his ___purple___ bandits, ___listening___ his henchmen, and
    ADJECTIVE   VERB ENDING IN "ING"

___Reading___ all the ne'er-do-wells. It was a/an ___trying___
VERB ENDING IN "ING"   ADJECTIVE

job, but someone had to ___talk___ it. Then the sheriff and
                          VERB

Deputy John put their ___knees___ to thinking about
                      PART OF THE BODY (PLURAL)

more ___dim___ problems.
     ADJECTIVE

"Who should we roust now, Deputy John?" asked the sheriff one

evening as they sat inside (the) ___White House___. Deputy John pointed
                                  A PLACE

at the wall of wanted ___coral Reefs___.
                      PLURAL NOUN

"Rustlin' Randy," he said. "He's one of Wild Bob's top leaders and

the head of the Roamin' Rustlers, a gang of ornery, lowdown

___cats___."
ANIMAL (PLURAL)

MAD LIBS® is fun to play with friends, but you can also play it by yourself! To begin with, DO NOT look at the chapter on the next page. Fill in the blanks on this page with the words called for. Then, using the words you have selected, fill in the blank spaces in the chapter.

Now you've created your own hilarious MAD LIBS® game!

CHAPTER 10:
THE ROAMIN' RUSTLERS

VERB (PAST TENSE) _____

ANIMAL (PLURAL) _____

NOUN _____

VERB ENDING IN "ING" _____

ADJECTIVE _____

PLURAL NOUN _____

NOUN _____

PLURAL NOUN _____

ANIMAL (PLURAL) _____

PLURAL NOUN _____

VERB ENDING IN "ING" _____

NOUN _____

SILLY WORD _____

NOUN _____

A PLACE _____

EXCLAMATION _____

PART OF THE BODY _____

CHAPTER 10:
THE ROAMIN' RUSTLERS

The next morning, the sheriff and Deputy John ___WELT___
VERB (PAST TENSE)

out of Gopher Gulch on their _____CATS_____ and headed into
ANIMAL (PLURAL)

the Sierra ___Mom___ desert, toward the hideout of the
NOUN

___Running___ Rustlers.
VERB ENDING IN "ING"

"Keeping the town ___TUFFY___ is one thing," said Deputy John,
ADJECTIVE

"but if we want to keep the peace, we've got to go after all of Wild Bob's

___Scoops___ and bring 'em to ___book___." The Roamin'
PLURAL NOUN   _NOUN_

___Pencils___ were known for stealing dairy ___Cows___
PLURAL NOUN   _ANIMAL (PLURAL)_

from the ranchers outside of Gopher Gulch, robbing innocent

___Shoes___ on their way to town, and even ___Spitting___
PLURAL NOUN   _VERB ENDING IN "ING"_

the stagecoach. "I reckon Rustlin' Randy and his ___Kitten___ are
NOUN

holed up at the old Okey ___Ka-pow___ Corral," said Deputy John.
SILLY WORD

"Maybe we can catch 'em there."

The sheriff nodded as the sun put a gleam on her gold ___plate___.
NOUN

"Let's ride to the Okey Dokey ___store___, then! ___wow___!"
A PLACE   _EXCLAMATION_

"You took the words right out of my ___heel___," said Deputy
PART OF THE BODY

John. "Let's ride!"

MAD LIBS® is fun to play with friends, but you can also play it by yourself! To begin with, DO NOT look at the chapter on the next page. Fill in the blanks on this page with the words called for. Then, using the words you have selected, fill in the blank spaces in the chapter.

Now you've created your own hilarious MAD LIBS® game!

CHAPTER 11:
BUSHWHACKED

NUMBER _____

ADJECTIVE _____

PLURAL NOUN _____

VERB _____

ADJECTIVE _____

PLURAL NOUN _____

NOUN _____

PLURAL NOUN _____

ADJECTIVE _____

ANIMAL (PLURAL) _____

PART OF THE BODY _____

VERB _____

VERB ENDING IN "ING" _____

EXCLAMATION _____

VERB (PAST TENSE) _____

CHAPTER 11:
BUSHWHACKED

After riding __19__ miles, the sheriff and Deputy John came

NUMBER

to the entrance of Ghetlawst Canyon, a maze of __shiny__ trails

ADJECTIVE

with steep __moms__ that travelers were known to __run__

PLURAL NOUN · VERB

in. "I reckon this is a/an __dark__ hiding place for Rustlin' Randy

ADJECTIVE

and his gang of __lime dipping dots__," said Deputy John.

PLURAL NOUN

Suddenly, from behind them, they heard a loud __mug__ .

NOUN

Deputy John and the sheriff twisted around in their horse

__mugs__ and saw . . . two __furry__ -looking outlaws

PLURAL NOUN · ADJECTIVE

sitting on __cats__ , led by Rustlin' Randy himself. "Wild

ANIMAL (PLURAL)

Bob told you this wasn't over, stranger," said Randy as he pulled

down the bandana that hid his __eye__ . "This here's a

PART OF THE BODY

bush-__walk__ , so we'll be __running__ your horses

VERB · VERB ENDING IN "ING"

and taking you to Wild Bob himself."

" __Whoa__ ," said the sheriff quietly to Deputy John, and

EXCLAMATION

they both __ran__ their horses and rode into the canyon.

VERB (PAST TENSE)

"Git 'em!" hollered Randy to his gang.

MAD LIBS® is fun to play with friends, but you can also play it by yourself! To begin with, DO NOT look at the chapter on the next page. Fill in the blanks on this page with the words called for. Then, using the words you have selected, fill in the blank spaces in the chapter.

Now you've created your own hilarious MAD LIBS® game!

CHAPTER 12:
THE CHASE

VERB (PAST TENSE) _____

VERB _____

PLURAL NOUN _____

VERB (PAST TENSE) _____

VERB (PAST TENSE) _____

ADJECTIVE _____

NOUN _____

FIRST NAME _____

ANIMAL (PLURAL) _____

ADJECTIVE _____

PART OF THE BODY _____

A PLACE _____

ANIMAL (PLURAL) _____

PLURAL NOUN _____

EXCLAMATION _____

ADJECTIVE _____

TYPE OF BUILDING _____

ADJECTIVE _____

CHAPTER 12:
THE CHASE

_____

The sheriff and Deputy John _____ deeper into

VERB (PAST TENSE)

Ghetlawst Canyon, trying to out-_____ Rustlin' Randy and his

VERB

_____. They _____ around sharp corners

PLURAL NOUN ... VERB (PAST TENSE)

and _____ into dark passages, with the outlaws in

VERB (PAST TENSE)

_____ pursuit. "You never told me your _____," said

ADJECTIVE ... NOUN

Deputy John. The sheriff turned to him and said, "_____."

FIRST NAME

Moments later, the sheriff and Deputy John rode their

_____ into a/an _____ clearing at the

ANIMAL (PLURAL) ... ADJECTIVE

_____ of the canyon. In the middle of the clearing, there

PART OF THE BODY

was a/an _____, surrounded by a fence, where hundreds of

A PLACE

_____ were being held. "They musta' stolen all of them

ANIMAL (PLURAL)

_____," said Deputy John.

PLURAL NOUN

"_____, _____ cattle rustlers," sneered the

EXCLAMATION ... ADJECTIVE

sheriff. The sheriff set her sights on an old _____ at the

TYPE OF BUILDING

center of the corral. Then she steered her horse toward the barn and

Deputy John followed. "We'll make our _____ stand in

ADJECTIVE

there," she said.

MAD LIBS® is fun to play with friends, but you can also play it by yourself! To begin with, DO NOT look at the chapter on the next page. Fill in the blanks on this page with the words called for. Then, using the words you have selected, fill in the blank spaces in the chapter.

Now you've created your own hilarious MAD LIBS® game!

CHAPTER 13:
TROUBLE AT THE OKEY DOKEY CORRAL

ADVERB _____

VERB ENDING IN "ING" _____

NOUN _____

NUMBER _____

VERB (PAST TENSE) _____

VERB _____

NOUN _____

ADJECTIVE _____

A PLACE _____

VERB _____

ADVERB _____

PART OF THE BODY (PLURAL) _____

NOUN _____

ADVERB _____

NOUN _____

EXCLAMATION _____

CHAPTER 13:
TROUBLE AT THE
OKEY DOKEY CORRAL

The sheriff and Deputy John rode inside the barn and _slowly_
ADVERB
locked the doors behind them. Moments later, the outlaws started

running on the barn doors. "Come on out!" yelled
VERB ENDING IN "ING"
Rustlin' Randy. "We've got a/an _cat_ to settle with you,
NOUN
sheriff, on account of you embarrassed Wild Bob." Then, Rustlin'

Randy and his _2_ outlaws _ran_ through
NUMBER   VERB (PAST TENSE)
the barn doors, ready to _walk_. But when they got inside
VERB
the barn . . . it was empty—except for the _chair_ on the
NOUN
ground. Rustlin' Randy, who wasn't the most _fuzzy_ tool in
ADJECTIVE
(the) _house_, was confused. "Now where'd they vamoose to?"
A PLACE

"_Speedwalk_ the rope, Deputy!" yelled the sheriff. Deputy John
VERB
swiftly pulled a rope that was slung over a beam above the
ADVERB
outlaws' _eyes_. On the other end of the long
PART OF THE BODY (PLURAL)
blanket was a lasso hidden by the hay on the floor of the barn.
NOUN
The lasso _quickly_ tightened around the outlaws and lifted them
ADVERB
up in the _Magazine_.
NOUN

"_Oops_!" screamed Randy!
EXCLAMATION

MAD LIBS® is fun to play with friends, but you can also play it by yourself! To begin with, DO NOT look at the chapter on the next page. Fill in the blanks on this page with the words called for. Then, using the words you have selected, fill in the blank spaces in the chapter.

Now you've created your own hilarious MAD LIBS® game!

CHAPTER 14:
BECOMING AN OUTLAW

ANIMAL (PLURAL) _____

PLURAL NOUN _____

EXCLAMATION _____

ADJECTIVE _____

COLOR _____

ARTICLE OF CLOTHING _____

NOUN _____

NUMBER _____

ARTICLE OF CLOTHING (PLURAL) _____

VERB _____

TYPE OF EVENT _____

SILLY WORD _____

VERB (PAST TENSE) _____

ARTICLE OF CLOTHING _____

NOUN _____

CHAPTER 14:
BECOMING AN OUTLAW

Rustlin' Randy and his outlaws dangled from the ceiling, angrier

than a bag of _____ in a roomful of _____ .
　　　　　　　　 ANIMAL (PLURAL)　　　　　　　　　PLURAL NOUN

"_____ ! Now how will we get to Wild Bob's secret meeting
　EXCLAMATION

on Mystery Mesa?" blurted Randy.

"_____ Mesa, you say?" said Deputy John.
　ADJECTIVE

"Oops," said Randy as he turned bright _____ . The sheriff
　　　　　　　　　　　　　　　　　　　　　　　　COLOR

reached up and took off Randy's _____ . She had a
　　　　　　　　　　　　　　　　ARTICLE OF CLOTHING

plan up her _____ .
　　　　　　　 NOUN

"Aw, c'mon," said Randy, "if you take our bandanas, you might as

well take our _____-gallon _____ , too."
　　　　　　　 NUMBER　　　　　ARTICLE OF CLOTHING (PLURAL)

"Good idea," replied John. "Me and the sheriff are going to

_____ up in your duds and infiltrate Wild Bob's secret
　VERB

_____ disguised as y'all."
　TYPE OF EVENT

"_____ ," hissed Randy, "Wild Bob won't be fooled by that."
　SILLY WORD

The sheriff _____ Randy's _____
　　　　　　　 VERB (PAST TENSE)　　　　　　　ARTICLE OF CLOTHING

around her face. The outlaw went silent in amazement. "Well I'll be,"

said Randy. "It's like looking in a/an _____ ."
　　　　　　　　　　　　　　　　　　　　 NOUN

From TALES FROM MAD LIBS®: THE GOOD, THE BAD, AND THE ITCHY
Copyright © 2020 by Penguin Random House LLC.

MAD LIBS® is fun to play with friends, but you can also play it by yourself! To begin with, DO NOT look at the chapter on the next page. Fill in the blanks on this page with the words called for. Then, using the words you have selected, fill in the blank spaces in the chapter.

Now you've created your own hilarious MAD LIBS® game!

CHAPTER 15:
THE BALLAD OF GOPHER GULCH, PART 3

NOUN _____

ADJECTIVE _____

NOUN _____

PART OF THE BODY (PLURAL) _____

VERB (PAST TENSE) _____

NOUN _____

ANIMAL (PLURAL) _____

NOUN _____

OCCUPATION _____

OCCUPATION _____

ADVERB _____

PLURAL NOUN _____

ADJECTIVE _____

NOUN _____

CHAPTER 15:
THE BALLAD OF GOPHER GULCH, PART 3

Warmed by the flames of the _____Lego_____ , the cowboys waited
NOUN

for the _____mad_____ cowgirl to continue her _____Carpet_____ . Their
ADJECTIVE   NOUN

bloodshot _____buttcheeks_____ were wide in anticipation. "What
PART OF THE BODY (PLURAL)

_____looked_____ next?" asked one cowboy. "Yeah, did the sheriff
VERB (PAST TENSE)

and Deputy John sneak into the outlaws' _____pillow_____ ?" asked
NOUN

another.

The gritty cowgirl smiled. "Hold your _____monsters_____ , I'm
ANIMAL (PLURAL)

getting there. Let me continue this here _____boy_____ . . ."
NOUN

The _____plumber_____ and _____farmer_____
OCCUPATION   OCCUPATION

rode _____at_____ and fast,
ADVERB

both dressed as _____carpets_____
PLURAL NOUN

and hoping to pass.

But Wild Bob was _____weird_____ ,
ADJECTIVE

and Wild Bob was mad,

and if he got half a/an _____T-Rex_____ ,
NOUN

well, things would get real bad.

MAD LIBS® is fun to play with friends, but you can also play it by yourself! To begin with, DO NOT look at the chapter on the next page. Fill in the blanks on this page with the words called for. Then, using the words you have selected, fill in the blank spaces in the chapter.

Now you've created your own hilarious MAD LIBS® game!

CHAPTER 16:
AT MYSTERY MESA

ADJECTIVE _____

ANIMAL (PLURAL) _____

PLURAL NOUN _____

ADJECTIVE _____

PART OF THE BODY _____

ADJECTIVE _____

ADJECTIVE _____

VERB ENDING IN "ING" _____

VERB (PAST TENSE) _____

ADJECTIVE _____

ADJECTIVE _____

NUMBER _____

ADJECTIVE _____

NOUN _____

NOUN _____

CHAPTER 16:
AT MYSTERY MESA

Once at _____ Mesa, the sheriff and Deputy John snuck in
           ADJECTIVE

to the crowd of outlaws who rode their _____ into a
                                        ANIMAL (PLURAL)

secret tunnel hidden behind some spiky _____. "Hey there,
                                         PLURAL NOUN

Rustlin' Randy!" yelled one outlaw, who had a/an _____
                                                    ADJECTIVE

mustache and a patch on his _____. "How's the
                             PART OF THE BODY

rustling business?"

"_____," said the sheriff, doing her _____ Rustlin'
   ADJECTIVE   ADJECTIVE

Randy impression.

"Same ol' _____ Randy," said the outlaw, before he
           VERB ENDING IN "ING"

_____ the sheriff on the back. "Always with the
 VERB (PAST TENSE)

_____ remarks!"
 ADJECTIVE

Then, the sheriff and Deputy John exited the tunnel. Above them,

they could see the _____ sky. They were on top of the mesa,
                    ADJECTIVE

surrounded by over _____ wild and _____, no-good,
                    NUMBER   ADJECTIVE

low-down outlaws. And in front of them, standing on a rock that

looked like a/an _____, was none other than the head
                  NOUN

_____ himself—Wild Bob!
 NOUN

MAD LIBS® is fun to play with friends, but you can also play it by yourself! To begin with, DO NOT look at the chapter on the next page. Fill in the blanks on this page with the words called for. Then, using the words you have selected, fill in the blank spaces in the chapter.

Now you've created your own hilarious MAD LIBS® game!

CHAPTER 17:
WILD BOB'S PLAN

PLURAL NOUN _____

NOUN _____

PART OF THE BODY (PLURAL) _____

NUMBER _____

ARTICLE OF CLOTHING (PLURAL) _____

ADJECTIVE _____

NOUN _____

VERB (PAST TENSE) _____

ANIMAL _____

NOUN _____

OCCUPATION _____

VERB _____

NOUN _____

PART OF THE BODY _____

SAME PART OF THE BODY _____

EXCLAMATION _____

CHAPTER 17:
WILD BOB'S PLAN

"My fellow _____," said Wild Bob as he addressed his

       PLURAL NOUN

bandits, "we've got a big _____ on our _____,

         NOUN   PART OF THE BODY (PLURAL)

and it's that no-good sheriff! It's time we got rid of that goody

_____-_____ for good!" The sheriff and

NUMBER   ARTICLE OF CLOTHING (PLURAL)

deputy exchanged _____ looks. It was time they made a hasty

           ADJECTIVE

_____!

NOUN

But when the sheriff _____ her horse to leave, Wild

         VERB (PAST TENSE)

Bob called out, "Randy, where do you think you're going? And since

when do you wear your hair in a/an _____-tail?" The sheriff

         ANIMAL

realized they had been caught.

"You're under _____," she yelled as she tore off her disguise.

       NOUN

The deputy did the same. "Surrender and we'll guarantee you a fair

trial in front of the _____."

      OCCUPATION

Wild Bob cackled. "I don't _____ so. I think *you'll* be facing

       VERB

an unfair _____ right here!" The sheriff and deputy stopped

   NOUN

their horses _____-to-_____ as Wild Bob's

PART OF THE BODY   SAME PART OF THE BODY

bandits crept closer and closer. "_____!" yelped the deputy.

        EXCLAMATION

MAD LIBS® is fun to play with friends, but you can also play it by yourself! To begin with, DO NOT look at the chapter on the next page. Fill in the blanks on this page with the words called for. Then, using the words you have selected, fill in the blank spaces in the chapter.

Now you've created your own hilarious MAD LIBS® game!

CHAPTER 18:
ESCAPE TO GOPHER GULCH

ADJECTIVE _____

NUMBER _____

VERB _____

NOUN _____

LETTER OF THE ALPHABET _____

VERB (PAST TENSE) _____

NOUN _____

NOUN _____

PART OF THE BODY (PLURAL) _____

NOUN _____

EXCLAMATION _____

VERB (PAST TENSE) _____

NOUN _____

VERB (PAST TENSE) _____

ANIMAL (PLURAL) _____

PLURAL NOUN _____

NOUN _____

CHAPTER 18:
ESCAPE TO GOPHER GULCH

"We're in kind of a/an _____ spot here," whispered Deputy
_{ADJECTIVE}

John to the sheriff. "They got us outnumbered _____ to one.
_{NUMBER}

We can't _____ all of 'em."
_{VERB}

The sheriff knew they had to come up with a/an _____ .
_{NOUN}

"Plan _____ ," said the sheriff.
_{LETTER OF THE ALPHABET}

"If you say so," said Deputy John as the outlaws _____
_{VERB (PAST TENSE)}

closer . . . and closer. At the last possible _____ , the sheriff
_{NOUN}

and deputy rode side-_____ in a circle, dragging
_{NOUN}

their _____ in the dirt and creating a huge
_{PART OF THE BODY (PLURAL)}

dust _____ . The bandits all coughed and yelled,
_{NOUN}

"_____!" In the confusion, the sheriff and deputy
_{EXCLAMATION}

_____ away from the outlaws and into the
_{VERB (PAST TENSE)}

_____ that led out of Mystery Mesa. Once outside, the duo
_{NOUN}

_____ away on their _____ .
_{VERB (PAST TENSE)}   _{ANIMAL (PLURAL)}

"Git 'em!" shouted Wild Bob as he and the other _____
_{PLURAL NOUN}

pursued the sheriff and Deputy John across the desert toward

Gopher _____ .
_{NOUN}

MAD LIBS® is fun to play with friends, but you can also play it by yourself! To begin with, DO NOT look at the chapter on the next page. Fill in the blanks on this page with the words called for. Then, using the words you have selected, fill in the blank spaces in the chapter.

Now you've created your own hilarious MAD LIBS® game!

CHAPTER 19:
THE STANDOFF

PLURAL NOUN _____

VERB ENDING IN "ING" _____

NOUN _____

TYPE OF FOOD _____

VERB ENDING IN "ING" _____

FIRST NAME _____

VERB (PAST TENSE) _____

ANIMAL (PLURAL) _____

EXCLAMATION _____

ADJECTIVE _____

NOUN _____

VERB (PAST TENSE) _____

PART OF THE BODY _____

PLURAL NOUN _____

COLOR _____

ADJECTIVE _____

VERB _____

CHAPTER 19:
THE STANDOFF

The sheriff and Deputy John rode back to Gopher Gulch faster

than a pair of _____, where the townsfolk were all
                PLURAL NOUN

_____ around a long _____ covered in
VERB ENDING IN "ING"   NOUN

_____ pies.
TYPE OF FOOD

"Howdy, Sheriff," said the mayor. "You made it back just in time for

our annual pie-_____ contest! By the way, how'd
                VERB ENDING IN "ING"

things go with Wild _____?" Deputy John pointed
                    FIRST NAME

behind him as Wild Bob and his men _____ into
                                    VERB (PAST TENSE)

town like a pack of angry _____. The mayor yelped,
                          ANIMAL (PLURAL)

"_____! That _____, huh?" Then the citizens
    EXCLAMATION   ADJECTIVE

scrambled for _____ as Wild Bob _____
              NOUN   VERB (PAST TENSE)

from his horse and stood face-to-_____ with the sheriff.
                                  PART OF THE BODY

"I think it's time we settled our _____," sneered Wild Bob.
                                  PLURAL NOUN

The sheriff picked up a pie. "How about we do it with these

_____-berry pies? Or are you afraid I'll embarrass you *again*?"
COLOR

"That's pretty _____ talk," said Wild Bob, "but can you
               ADJECTIVE

_____ it up?" Wild Bob picked up a pie, too. It was a standoff.
VERB

MAD LIBS® is fun to play with friends, but you can also play it by yourself! To begin with, DO NOT look at the chapter on the next page. Fill in the blanks on this page with the words called for. Then, using the words you have selected, fill in the blank spaces in the chapter.

Now you've created your own hilarious MAD LIBS® game!

CHAPTER 20:
THE DUEL

TYPE OF FOOD _____

NUMBER _____

EXCLAMATION _____

PART OF THE BODY _____

VERB (PAST TENSE) _____

PART OF THE BODY _____

VERB (PAST TENSE) _____

PLURAL NOUN _____

EXCLAMATION _____

ADJECTIVE _____

A PLACE _____

PLURAL NOUN _____

EXCLAMATION _____

ADJECTIVE _____

TYPE OF EVENT _____

NOUN _____

VERB (PAST TENSE) _____

NOUN _____

CHAPTER 20:
THE DUEL

_____

Holding their fresh _____ pies, the sheriff and Wild Bob
                    TYPE OF FOOD

turned away from each other and counted paces. "Five, four,

_____, two, one! _____!" Wild Bob yelled before
   NUMBER   EXCLAMATION

he turned and threw his pie at the sheriff's _____. But the
                                          PART OF THE BODY

sheriff _____ out of the way and threw her pie, scoring
        VERB (PAST TENSE)

a direct hit on Wild Bob's _____. The sheriff
                              PART OF THE BODY

_____! Then, all the _____ of Gopher
VERB (PAST TENSE)   PLURAL NOUN

Gulch let out a hearty "_____!" Seeing their leader
                         EXCLAMATION

humiliated, Wild Bob's gang _____-tailed it right out of
                             ADJECTIVE

town as Deputy John took Wild Bob into (the) _____ to lock
                                              A PLACE

him up behind _____ once and for all. "_____,"
               PLURAL NOUN   EXCLAMATION

grumbled Wild Bob.

That evening, Gopher Gulch celebrated Wild Bob's defeat with

a/an _____ _____. But it was time for this stranger-
     ADJECTIVE   TYPE OF EVENT

turned-sheriff to turn in her _____ and move on. So, she left
                              NOUN

her badge on Deputy John's desk and _____ her horse
                                      VERB (PAST TENSE)

toward the setting _____.
                    NOUN

MAD LIBS® is fun to play with friends, but you can also play it by yourself! To begin with, DO NOT look at the chapter on the next page. Fill in the blanks on this page with the words called for. Then, using the words you have selected, fill in the blank spaces in the chapter.

Now you've created your own hilarious MAD LIBS® game!

CHAPTER 21:
THE LAST BALLAD OF GOPHER GULCH

NOUN _____

VERB (PAST TENSE) _____

ANIMAL _____

SILLY WORD _____

ADJECTIVE _____

VERB _____

NOUN _____

PLURAL NOUN _____

NOUN _____

VERB ENDING IN "ING" _____

PLURAL NOUN _____

ADJECTIVE _____

NOUN _____

CHAPTER 21:
THE LAST BALLAD OF GOPHER GULCH

The cowboys fell silent as the gritty cowgirl finished her

_____ . The fire _____ , and somewhere far off
  NOUN   VERB (PAST TENSE)

in the desert, a/an _____ let out a lonely "_____."
                    ANIMAL   SILLY WORD

"Well, if that wasn't the _____-tootinest story I ever did
                       ADJECTIVE

_____ ," said one cowboy.
  VERB

"And every last _____ of it is true," said the cowgirl.
            NOUN

Curious, one of the _____ asked her, "What's your name,
             PLURAL NOUN

cowgirl?"

The cowgirl turned, swinging her long pony-_____ in the
                          NOUN

night breeze. "You can call me . . . *the stranger.*" Then she walked into

the darkness, _____ as she went . . .
           VERB ENDING IN "ING"

So many _____ ago,
           PLURAL NOUN

these _____ things did occur.
       ADJECTIVE

Call me stranger or sheriff,

either way, I was her.

The _____
      NOUN

Join the millions of Mad Libs fans creating wacky and wonderful stories on our apps!

Download Mad Libs today!